WALK
ON THE
WILD
SIDE

To Jasper, Freddie and Maggie

Text and illustrations © 2015 Nicholas Oldland

This edition is only available for distribution through the school market by
Scholastic Canada Book Fairs and Book Clubs.

ISBN 978-1-77138-544-2

CM PA 15 0 9 8 7 6 5 4 3 2 1

Kids Can Press acknowledges the financial support of the Government of
Ontario, through the Ontario Media Development Corporation's Ontario Book
Initiative; the Ontario Arts Council; the Canada Council for the Arts; and the
Government of Canada, through the CBF, for our publishing activity.

Published in Canada by	Published in the U.S. by
Kids Can Press Ltd.	Kids Can Press Ltd.
25 Dockside Drive	2250 Military Road
Toronto, ON M5A 0B5	Tonawanda, NY 14150

www.kidscanpress.com

The artwork in this book was rendered in Photoshop.
The text is set in Animated Gothic.

Edited by Yvette Ghione
Series design by Marie Bartholomew
Designed by Julia Naimska

The hardcover edition of this book is smyth sewn casebound.
The paperback edition of this book is limp sewn with a drawn-on cover.
Manufactured in Malaysia in 10/2014 by Tien Wah Press (Pte) Ltd.

CM 15 0 9 8 7 6 5 4 3 2 1

Library and Archives Canada Cataloguing in Publication

Oldland, Nicholas, 1972–, author, illustrator
Walk on the wild side / Nicholas Oldland.
(Life in the wild)

ISBN 978-1-77138-109-3 (bound)

I. Title. II. Series.

PS8629.L46W35 2014   jC813'.6   C2013-908163-1

Kids Can Press is a [orus™ Entertainment company

WALK
ON THE
WILD
SIDE

Nicholas Oldland

Kids Can Press

There once was a bear, a moose and a beaver who loved adventure. But sometimes their competitive natures got in the way of having fun.

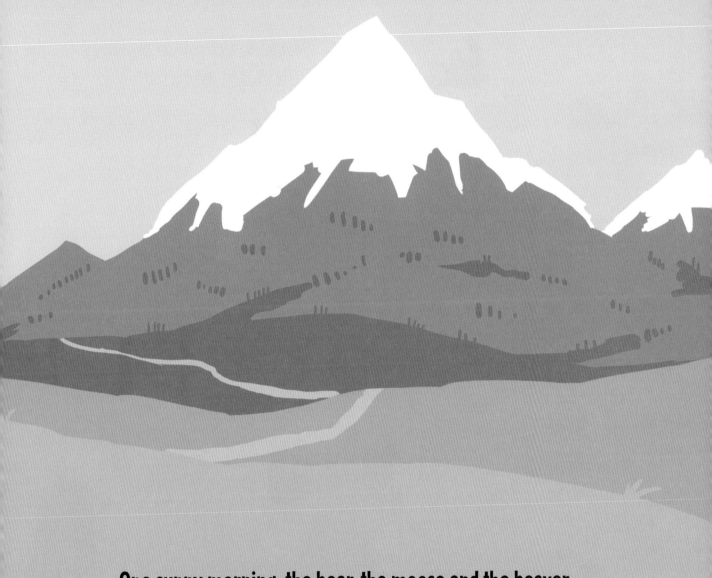

One sunny morning, the bear, the moose and the beaver decided it was a great day to climb a mountain.

To get to the mountain, they descended into a valley ...

Walked through a grassy field ...

ARE WE THERE YET?

Waded through a stream ...

And crossed a deep canyon.

DON'T LOOK DOWN.

At the foot of the mountain, they stopped for a snack. Between mouthfuls, the bear, the moose and the beaver discussed ways to make their hike more interesting.

The beaver thought the best way to add some excitement was to make it a race.

As soon as they finished their last bites, the three friends were off and running. The race was on!

Thanks to his long legs, the moose took an early lead. But the beaver and the bear followed right on his tail.

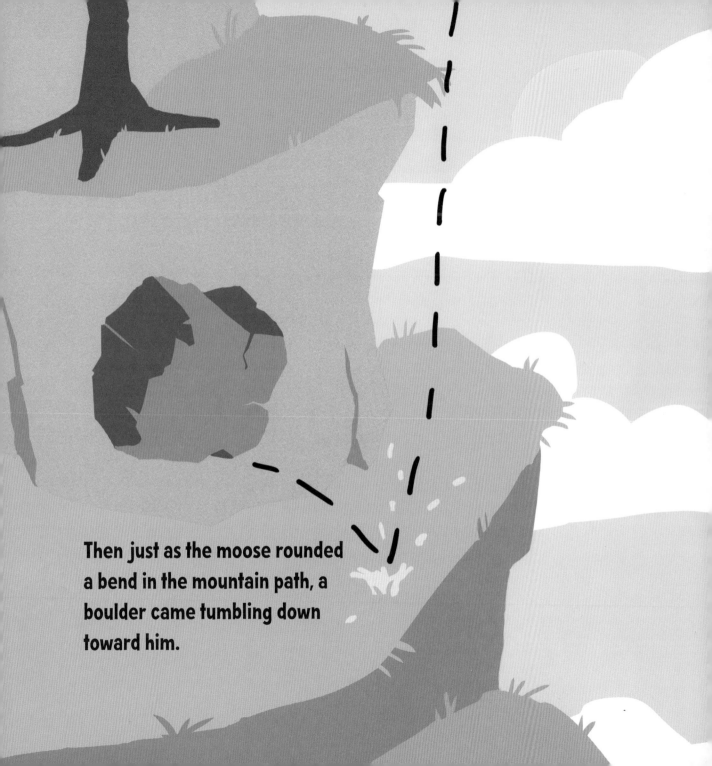

Then just as the moose rounded a bend in the mountain path, a boulder came tumbling down toward him.

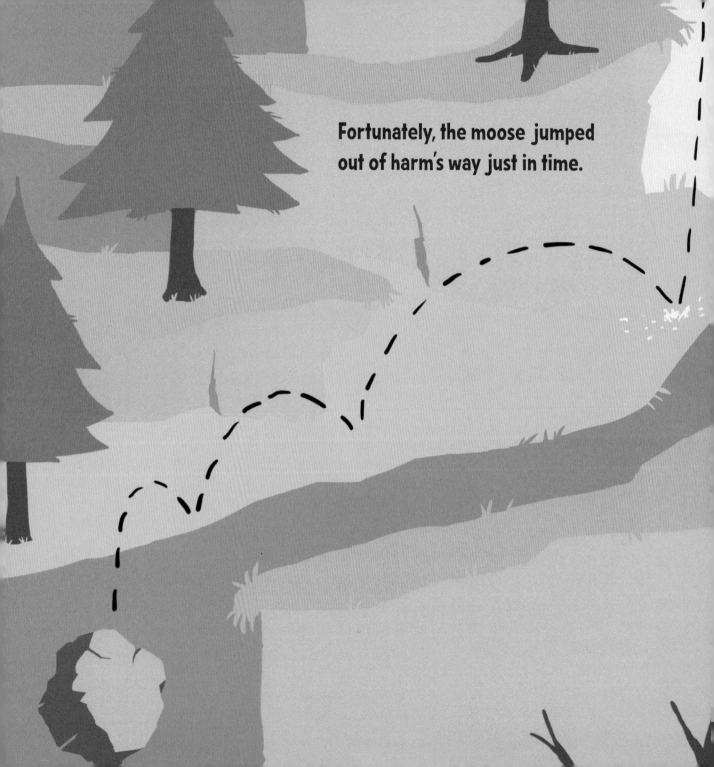

Fortunately, the moose jumped out of harm's way just in time.

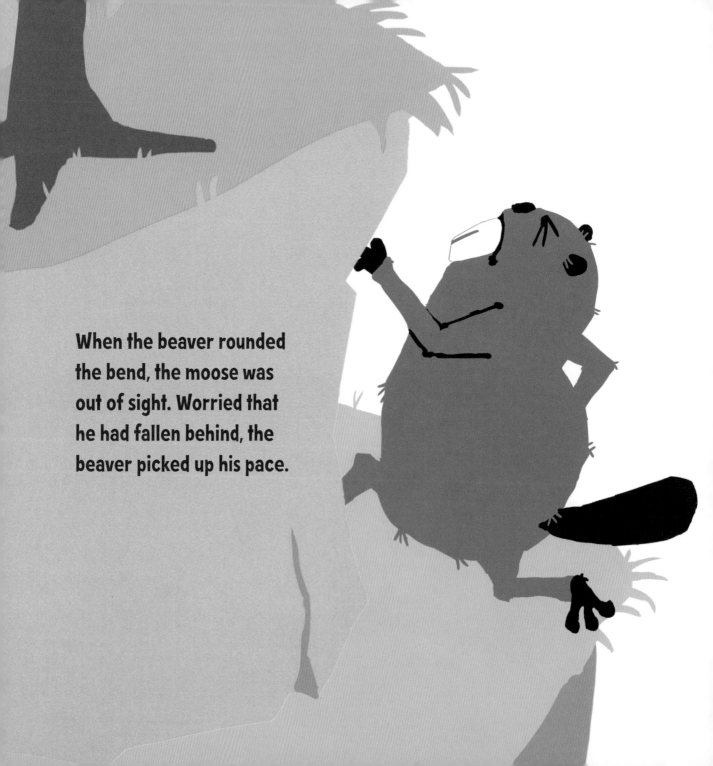

When the beaver rounded the bend, the moose was out of sight. Worried that he had fallen behind, the beaver picked up his pace.

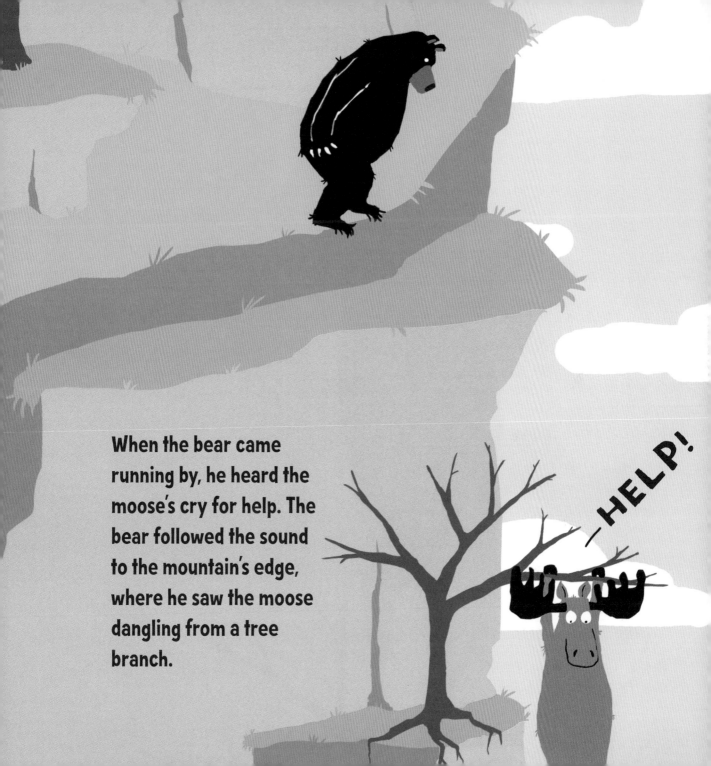

When the bear came running by, he heard the moose's cry for help. The bear followed the sound to the mountain's edge, where he saw the moose dangling from a tree branch.

HELP!

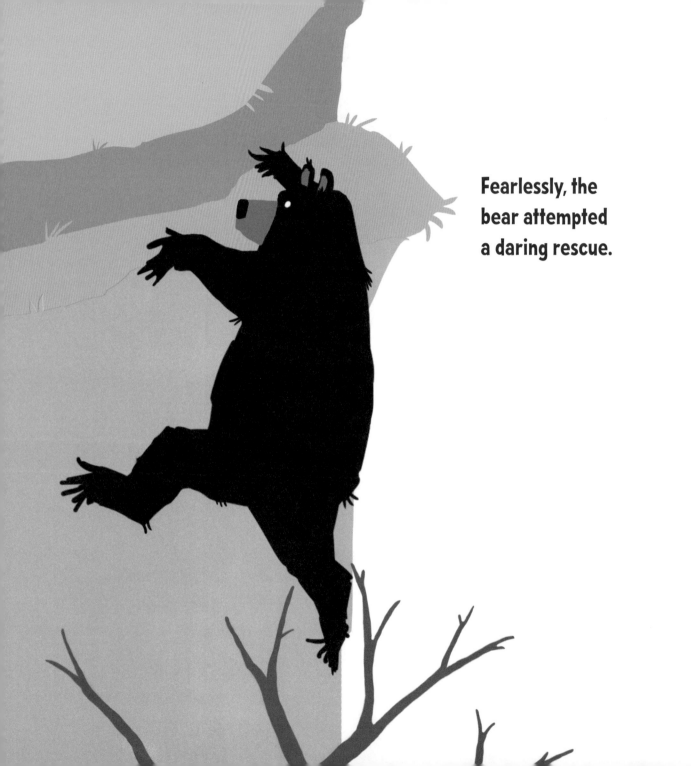

Fearlessly, the bear attempted a daring rescue.

Thanks to the moose's quick reflexes, the bear's life was saved.

THANKS!

But now they were both hanging on for their lives.

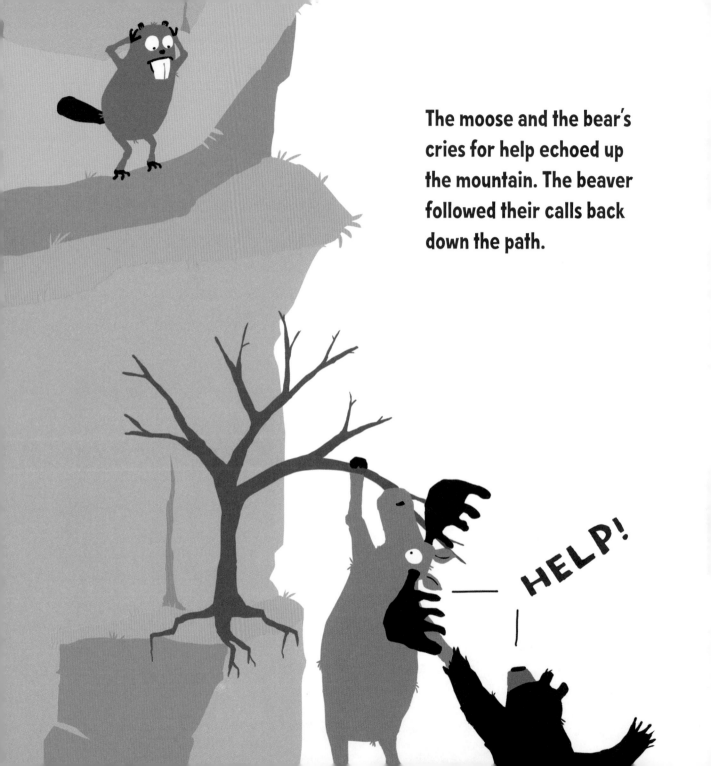

The moose and the bear's cries for help echoed up the mountain. The beaver followed their calls back down the path.

HELP!

The beaver's instincts kicked in.

He chewed down a tree ...

Carved out a few notches ...

ARGHHH!

And lowered the simple ladder to the moose and the bear so they could climb up.

Back on solid ground, the three friends realized their hike had become a little too exciting. If they were going to make it to the top of the mountain, a slower pace might be better.

And that's when their hike became truly interesting.

They explored a dark cave ...

Discovered a prehistoric fossil ...

And helped one another
along the way.

At the end of the day, the bear, the moose and the beaver
agreed that reaching the top of the mountain was great,
but enjoying the journey together was even better.